90 Days Of Summer

A Memoir

by

Phil Cronkhite

with Lioness DeWinter

Lulu Author

ISBN: 978-1-300-58284-7

For my beautiful wife, Winona.

I love you.

90 Days Of Summer

School is out! Now we could do the things young boys have been thinking about all winter. We all got up early, and after a hearty breakfast we took off to the river, which was about half a mile from our house.

First thing to do was to get ready to catch some fish. Junior had all the fixings: line and fish hooks, for a trout line which was about 25 feet. Then he put hooks on about every three feet, and lastly the bait (angleworms, which we dug up the night before) and placed the baited line out into the river.

We'd have to be back to check the line before we returned to the house for the evening, but for now, we were headed to the river! Romping, running, what a great day! After about an hour, it was time for a swim. We all removed our clothes, neatly stacking them away from the water, and collectively made a mad dash for the river--Wow! What a treat! I was kind of little, so I just stayed in the shallows while the others ventured out into the deeper water.

Two hours later, it was time to lay on the sand, look at the clouds, and dream...

Well, as you know, boys can't stay still very long, when there's a whole world to explore, so up we went! We walked and walked, further and further, looking for new adventures. By then, it was 'round about lunchtime, so we headed home to eat before we were off once again to the river.

We checked the trout line--we had two fish on it, how about that for a first try!--then we took the fish off the hooks, and put them into some water to keep them fresh before baiting the hooks once more and throwing them back into the water.

So off we went again, happy to be outdoors, doing nothing.

We decided to take another swim--we had to be the cleanest kids around!--and we spent the rest of the day just exploring the river beds, the stream, and just sitting in the shade of the trees along the river bank.

The sun was getting low, so it was time to be heading home for the evening. We checked the fish line once again, and believe it or not, we had two more catfish on the line! Junior took them off, strung them up, baited the hook again, and tossed it back into the river to be checked upon our return, the next morning. We headed back home with our four catfish, pretty proud kids! That would be our supper the next day.

Junior, being the oldest, would clean them and have them all ready for the frying pan. Four little boys--what a wonderful day it was! We were all tired out and ready for supper, and a few minutes later we went off to bed--no trouble getting to sleep; we were worn out, but oh so happy!

Before we go any further, let's back up and get caught up with what this story is all about. I grew up in rural Oklahoma, my brothers, my sister Shirley, and me, Phil.

The oldest brother was Junior. He was our mentor, and we all looked up to him. He had learned much from our Dad and Uncles, about the things that all boys should know about hunting and fishing and the great outdoors.

The next brother was Don. He was the worker. He had to do all the heavy work around the farm, and was able to do most everything on our outdoor excursions.

The third one was J.T. He was the one that could get into trouble doing nothing, but he was lots of fun!

I was the littlest one of the four at the time of the story, although we did have a little sister, Shirley, and a baby brother, Cy. The others took care of me, and I never had a worry in the whole, big world. It sure was nice! I miss those carefree days.

We had all finished school for the year.

In my town, we all went to the same school. It was a one-room country school that included grades one through eight. We all learned from each other that way!

We also had a tiny little sister that we had to take care of. We protected her, but she wasn't quite old enough to accompany us on our afternoon trips through the woods and lakes. We also had a baby brother, Cy.

We explored the woods and found many things to do, like climbing trees to get to the crows nests to gather eggs. Once we had our prize, we would pierce both ends of the eggs, blow out the yolks, and string them up on the wall of our little shed which we had transformed into our clubhouse. This is where we made our plans of what to do each day.

Junior had his fish lines, his traps, and pelts from the animals that he had caught.

Our farm was in the lowlands, but we also had a large pasture/ranch land up in the hills away from our house. It was too far to walk up there, so we rode our little pony, Joker. We went up the road about a mile, then through the draws (a creek with no water) on up another mile where we had some cattle and sometimes a herd of sheep, which needed care every day. Each of us had his turn.

One day, after checking the sheep and cows, and seeing that everything as all right, I was on my way back, and came upon our water tank. I needed to water Joker, anyhow, but a thought occurred to me...the water sure looked inviting!

After looking both ways, I took off all of my clothes and jumped in, forgetting one very important fact: I couldn't swim!!! Well, I sure learned in a hurry! This was a big tank, about thirty feet across and six feet deep! I was able to paddle from one side to the other, and I felt like a great big boy. I was very proud of myself!

I didn't say much to my folks about this later on, but they probably wondered why I was so clean!

It was time to head for home, to put Joker out for the day and to feed him his hay and oats. By then, it would be time for supper (which was the best meal of the day, and one we never missed). There was never any problem getting us to go to bed, as we were always really worn out. We needed our rest for our early morning chores, which included milking the cows.

In the morning, we would run the milk through the separator, which isolates the cream from the fresh milk. Then, we would have to feed the hogs. The pigs enjoyed the skim milk that was mixed into their mash. We would watch them eat for awhile, until it was time for breakfast. Our Mama Gertrude used to fix great breakfasts for us, with plenty of eggs and toast and cereal and we would sometimes enjoy a special treat of ham or bacon.

After breakfast, we would gather together to do our thing. We loved to camp and fish. We walked to the river, found a sand bar to walk across, although we found it hard to resist jumping in. The water was so clear that you could see the bottom, where the fish were swimming in and out of the moss.

We would make a day of it before heading home to milk the cows and finish our remaining chores before supper. After that, we would head out once more for the night. On a particularly exciting night, we found an abandoned rowboat, and took it out on the lake. We were rowing along enjoying ourselves, when--SURPRISE!--a 14-inch bass jumped up out of the water and landed right in the boat!

The bass made a nice evening snack for a pack of hungry boys. Junior lit a fire, and as the fish cooked, we stretched out and relaxed under the stars for a night's rest.

The next day, we had work to do around the farm. We welcomed our breakfast that morning, because we were some busy kids! Junior and Don had to get the horses ready to hook up to the cultivator to work the cotton fields. My brothers were not big boys, but they handled the horses like old 'hands. Even as small as I was, I had a job with the road maintenance department, which made me a bit of extra money. I had to cut down the weeds along the side of the road, one-half mile on each side. He paid me twenty-five cents for each side, which made me a cool fifty cents by noon. With this, I would buy school clothes for the upcoming year.

After a big early supper of steak and mashed potatoes with Mom's special white gravy and her homemade bread and butter, we were ready to take off again.

J.T. and I got our horses and decided to

ride to the nearest store, which was about one-and-a-half miles down the road.

Once there, J.T. decided that we should have something to smoke, so we bought a pack of Wings for ten cents, and a sack of Bull Durham for a nickel. Boy, we felt big and manly...mad, bad and dangerous to know! Hoo, yeah!

I had to pitch in for them, but J.T. immediately staked a claim on the smoking supplies and put them in his pocket, away from the prying hands of his younger brother.

We immediately tried the Wings--which were ready made--but the Bull Durham we had to roll ourselves, and it took some practice to get that done!

J.T. smoked the biggest share of them, I guess. This was our first time smoking, so we didn't feel all that hot. We had to stop and rest under a tree for awhile before heading home.

Well, I'll tell ya, I had almost decided that this smoking stuff was for the birds, but later, J.T. decided to take me along to this big empty water tank on our property, where we resumed our smoking career once more, artfully hidden away from prying eyes. We were so clever...or so we thought. We didn't realize that the smoke would travel up and out like a chimney...signaling Daddy

Casey as effectively as a waving flag.

When we came out, he was waiting for us with a stern look upon his face.

Uh-oh.

Without a word, he marched us to the front porch, signaled for us to stay there, and returned with a carton of unfiltered Camel cigarettes.

"Smoke these until I tell you to stop," he ordered. His face was stern, but his eyes were kind and full of humor. My Daddy was a very good man.

Anyhow, this was the worst punishment

that he could have given us. Both of our skinny little butts were swaying on our feet, dizzy, cross-eyed and green to the gills by the third pack. When he saw that we had learned our lesson, he allowed us to stop and told us to go wash up for bed. We had plenty of work to do in the morning.

I dreamed of endless whirls of smoke, and I didn't touch another cigarette until I was seventeen.

The next day, we rode to the pasture to check the sheep, cattle and the work horses. Everything looked A-OK until we spotted some turkey buzzards circling overhead. Shortly afterwards, we found the remains of a little lamb that had been killed by the wild coyotes. The buzzards were cleaning up the remains, or "leftovers", as my brothers called it. Its an amazing and beautiful thing--nature--how it takes care of itself that way.

We didn't see any more coyotes, so we headed back to the house for some much-needed dinner. This was a Saturday, so we had our favorite: Mama's corn bread, cooked navy beans, and a big piece of homemade chocolate cake for dessert. After that, we played all afternoon. We climbed trees and explored the great outdoors as usual.

Daddy got me up early the next morning. We had to go out and grade (level or smooth) some of the side roads for the county. It was a big job, about ten to twelve miles. We used a tractor to pull the grader, and Daddy let me drive. It was a really big job for such a little guy! I was very proud of myself.

On the way back, the sun had just risen, and the rest of the country was waking up all around. Crossing the road in front of us was a Mama skunk and her six little ones, following her as if in a parade. We stopped and watched them, as one straggled behind. He would never have caught up and would have been left to die, so I waited until the Mama skunk was a great distance away, then jumped down and scooped the tiny skunk up into my arms. He was very little, and (lucky for me) he didn't try to spray me. Skunks are such pretty animals, and this little one was tame, and more than happy to sit beside me in the tool box on the side of the tractor as we finished grading the road.

We finished the job by breakfast time, and Daddy and I got to sit and eat while the rest of the boys did the chores. Daddy built a cage for my new pet, so that he would have a place of his own.

"A hideout," my Pa called it.

I would go out and feed him and visit him, just like a little puppy. I named him Stinker, although he never did spray any of us. He lived with us for quite awhile, before he disappeared one day without a trace. It was hard on me, I'll admit. I was so fond of Stinker, and we were such good friends. However, being raised on a country farm, I knew in my heart that the best place for a wild animal was in its own territory, where it could truly be free.

We had many other wild pets throughout the years, but little Stinker was my favorite.

At this time of year, the cows, hogs and sheep had had their babies, which kept us pretty darn busy. Some of the lambs and the calves had to be bottle fed because their Moms had abandoned them, or they didn't have enough milk. We kids enjoyed the bottle feedings. It was a lot of fun to see the way that they'd go after the bottles, which were like baby bottles, only much larger.

The pigs were the most self-reliant, being very intelligent animals, and normally required only a few weeks of bottle-feedings before they would begin to forage for themselves. Very seldom would we lose any of the babies. They would all grow up to be nice pets and useful animals. The pigs were my favorites because they were playful and easy to care for. Junior liked the lambs and sheep, and raised them until the day he died. The little colts were frisky and so much fun to raise. We would train them for riding, and to help with the farm work.

The crops required a bit more attention. This was before people could afford the modern machinery we use today. We had to do much of the work with horses and mules, and we had hired hands to do the heavy work that we could not.

The men who worked for us had no idea of what they were getting themselves into, with a passel of ornery little boys around. One time, J.T. and I were exploring the field where one of the men was cultivating the cotton. It was a really hot, sultry day and he had to carry a jug of water which was wrapped in a burlap sack to keep it cool. He would go down one row of cotton and up another, then ever so often stop the horses, water them, and come get himself a drink.

We watched him do this for awhile, and then J.T. got a bright idea.

We caught some little frogs and put them in the jug of water that the farm hand had brought to drink from.

J.T. and I ducked out of sight, and waited for him to come back to the jug to take a drink...

Well, guess what--he took a big old gulp of it, and up and out jumped an explosion of little frogs!!! One jumped right into his mouth!

Ha! By then, he had figured out that he had been had--not that we didn't give it away as we rolled on the ground, clutching our guts and laughing so hard that we nearly wet our pants!--and he started toward us. We jumped up like a couple of rabbits and raced away. He could have caught us if he had wanted to, but we didn't give him much of a chance.

We didn't see him again until later that day at supper, and by that time, he had cooled down and had seen the humor of the situation. Phew! He just winked at us to let us know that he knew what we did, but he'd never admit that we'd put one over on him. Not in a million years. I still smile when I think about him.

Summer was winding down, and we

tried to find all the time that we can just to celebrate our time together as brothers. We went swimming and fishing in the river nearly every day. On this day, we sat by the clear waters and watched the sun perch as they nibbled the bait on our hooks. We caught quite a few that day, along with some catfish. It was a day I've always remembered: warm sunshine, and not a cloud in the bright, azure of the Oklahoma sky...

Anyhow, it was soon time to get our stuff together and head for home. It was nearly time for supper. With all those fish, we were able to feed all of us kids, Mama and Daddy, our little sister Shirley, and our baby brother, Cy, along with the hired hands.

~*~*~*~

After supper, it was off to bed. We didn't have television then. We had a radio, but it ran off of the car battery, so we didn't use it too much. We didn't have electricity, either. We had Cole oil lamps--which weren't really bright enough to read by--so we just closed our eyes and went to sleep. We would need the sleep, because in addition to the regular chores, there was something planned for the last weekend of the summer: a rodeo, and an American Indian celebration/pow wow.

What a weekend! Before the riding and roping in the rodeo portion of the gathering, they had tons of stuff for us kids to do. My favorite was the greased pig chase!!! They oiled down a big hog and all the kids took off after it, whooping and hollering. He was slick as snot, and even though I caught him, I couldn't hold on, so another kid ran him down and caught him. He got to keep the pig for his very own. I should have made sure to hold on when I had the chance, but it didn't spoil my fun. Instead, I tried my luck at climbing the greased flag pole. Unfortunately, I was too short and small to inch my way to the top. You can imagine how I looked with the grease all over me!

Later on, after we got cleaned up, the rodeo portion began. We had men from all of the ranches in the area who rode the horses and the steers and roped the calves. It was great fun for all of the families, a true community event.

After the rodeo, the pow wow began. The Cheyenne and Arapaho American Indians who lived on the reservation around us danced and celebrated. They put up their shelters, or tipis, and were dressed in their ceremonial finest. Back in the 1930s, it was a simpler time. We were the personification of the philosophy of our forefathers. We were a melting pot community, united in love. Everyone talked easily with each other. Black and white, red and yellow...we were not colors to one another. We were simply "Phil" and "John", "Kenneth" and "Casey" and "Gertrude". We celebrated one another, and connected in our hearts.

We danced around the fire that night--men, women, and children--all together. No barriers, no social stigma. We were all hardworking people, taking a break from our daily chores just to bask in the joy of our community. We circle danced together all weekend...the fire reaching for the night sky as we celebrated well into the night.

THE END

www.ingramcontent.com/pod-product-compliance
Ingram Content Group UK Ltd.
Pitfield, Milton Keynes, MK11 3LW, UK
UKHW041901190726
13854UKWH00003B/1024